OUR CAT HAS KITTENS

by Alan Trussell-Cullen

From the Library of

First published in 1990

Ashton Scholastic Limited
Private Bag 1, Penrose, Auckland 5, New Zealand.

Ashton Scholastic Pty Ltd
PO Box 579, Gosford, NSW 2250, Australia.

Scholastic Inc.
730 Broadway, New York, NY 10003, USA

Scholastic-TAB Publications Ltd
123 Newkirk Road, Richmond Hill, Ontario L4C 3G5, Canada.

Scholastic Publications Ltd
Marlborough House, Holly Walk, Leamington Spa, Warwickshire CV32 4LS, England

Copyright © Alan Trussell-Cullen, 1989

National Library of New Zealand
Cataloguing-in-Publication data

Trussell-Cullen, Alan.
Our cat has kittens / by Alan Trussell-Cullen. Auckland, N.Z.: Ashton
Scholastic, 1990.
1 v. (Read by reading)
Picture story book for children.
ISBN 1-86943-006-9
1. Readers—Cats. 2. Readers—Kittens. I. Title. II. Series:
Read by reading series
428.6 (NZ823.2)

5 4 3 2 1

Typeset in Garamond Light by Rennies Illustrations Ltd
Printed in Hong Kong

0 1 2 3 4 / 9

OUR CAT HAS KITTENS

by Alan Trussell-Cullen

READ BY READING

Ashton Scholastic

Auckland Sydney New York Toronto London

Spring was mating time for our cat, Njinska.

The tom cats seemed to come from all over the neighbourhood. We wondered which one would be the father of Njinska's kittens. Perhaps Njinska knew, but if she did, she wasn't telling.

A month went by. We began to notice that Njinska was changing. She was growing larger and larger as the kittens grew bigger and bigger inside her.

But that wasn't all. She'd always been a cat that liked to roam around but now she seemed to want to spend more time inside.

She began to act quite differently towards all the neighbours' cats, too. Whereas before she didn't seem to mind other cats wandering across our property, now she would growl and sometimes she would even run out and chase a neighbour's cat away. It was as if she were marking out her territory to ensure that the house and the garden would be safe for her kittens.

The weeks continued to pass: five weeks, six weeks, seven . . . Surely she would have the kittens soon? Sometimes when we stroked her belly we could feel the kittens moving about inside. How many kittens were there? Two? Three? Four?

Njinska began to act strangely. She climbed into boxes and squeezed behind beds. If we left a drawer open, she would climb inside and curl up on our clothes. She was looking for somewhere safe and cosy to keep her kittens when they were born. She wanted a 'nest'.

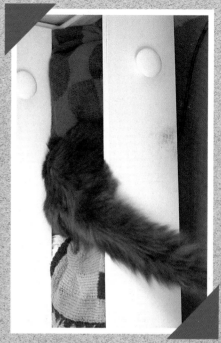

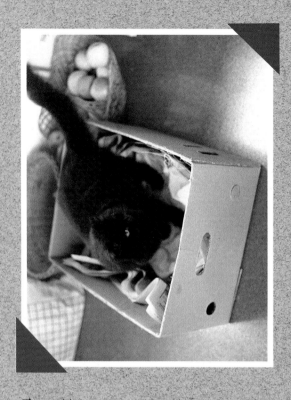

We asked the local shopkeeper for a cardboard box which we lined with newspaper and soft cloth. Then we let Njinska try it out. Yes, it seemed all right.

The vet told us that it usually took nine weeks before kittens are ready to be born. So when we thought that about nine weeks had passed, we watched Njinska anxiously.

One morning, Njinska climbed onto my bed and began to purr loudly. It was not like any purr we'd ever heard before. She's having her kittens at last, we thought. We moved her into her box with an old red blanket but she immediately climbed out again. She didn't seem to like the box being in the middle of the room, so we pushed it into the bottom of the wardrobe amongst our shoes and clothes. Njinska decided that this was much better.

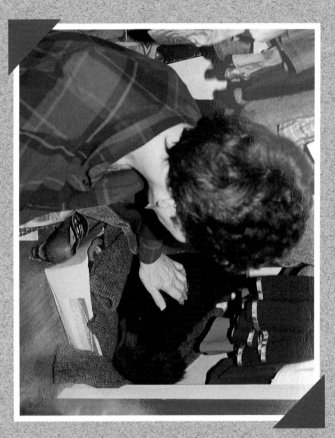

Njinska seemed to want us to stay close by so we took it in turns to sit with her, stroking and keeping watch. We could feel her abdomen tightening as her uterus gently squeezed the kittens into position ready to be born. After about three hours, we were beginning to wonder if the kittens would *ever* be born.

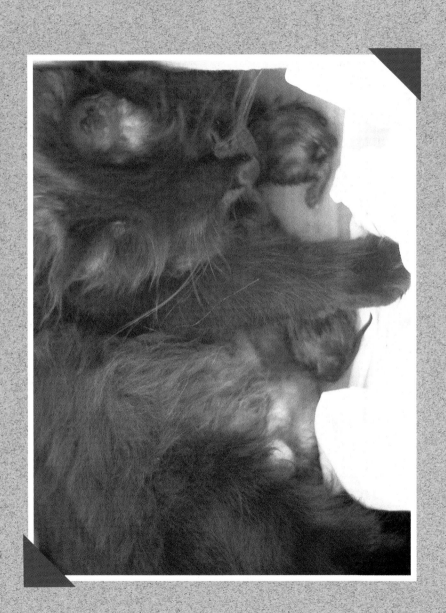

And then . . .
    A little black kitten came slithering out! It was all wet with its eyes shut tight and it was inside a kind of shiny, plastic-looking coating. The kitten was followed by the placenta. We knew that this was what supplied food and oxygen to the kittens while they were inside their mother. Njinska immediately began to lick off the coating covering the kitten. She ate the placenta and bit through the cord that connected it to the kitten.

No sooner had she cleaned up the first kitten, than another one was on its way. And another. However, we had to wait another hour before the last kitten was born.

That made four fine kittens. They all had their eyes shut but it didn't take them long to find Njinska's nipples and start to feed.

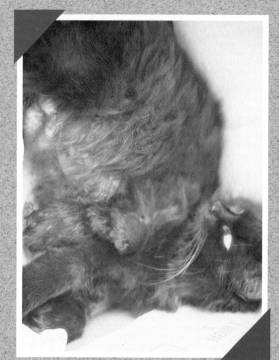

For the first ten days the kittens stayed in the box all the time. Their eyes were still closed and they spent the time either sleeping or feeding from Njinska.

On the tenth day, the little grey tabby kitten opened its eyes. Two days later they all had their eyes open and were beginning to try to clamber out of the box. At first they were very weak and clumsy. But gradually they became stronger and more determined to explore.

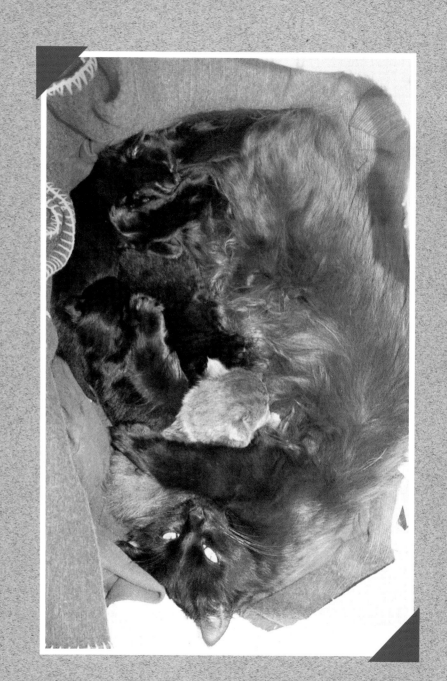

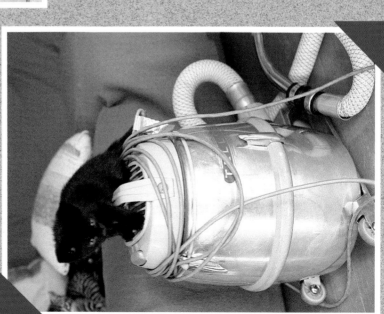

Three weeks had passed now and the kittens were spending more and more time out of the box. They were very curious about everything. They tried to climb into cupboards, and discovered many strange things, such as vacuum cleaners, newspapers and shoes . . . .

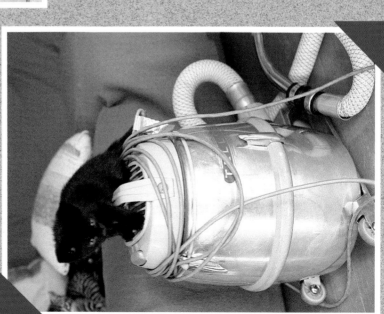

Whenever the kittens grew tired or hungry, they would return to Njinska. While they fed from her she would wash them and tidy up their fur. Then they would all settle down for a nap.

By the time they were four weeks old, the kittens were getting up to mischief. They played together, having mock fights and chasing each other around the house. Sometimes Njinska joined in with their games. All the time she was teaching them the things cats need to know. She taught them how to lap up milk from a saucer. Their first attempts to drink by themselves were disastrous. They kept putting their paws in the milk, much to their disgust. But soon they had mastered it.

Njinska was also teaching them how to stalk, how to pounce and how to fight — after all, cats are hunters. But obviously she felt that the kittens were not yet ready to go outside. If a kitten did manage to get out the door and down the steps, Njinska would pick it up by the scruff of its neck and carry it back inside.

Once the kittens were five weeks old, however, Njinska finally let them play outside. At first they were bewildered by all the strange new things. They didn't seem to like the feel of grass under their paws and jumped with fright whenever anything moved. But after a few hours outside, they were soon discovering all kinds of exciting things to play with. They found an old basket they could clamber into. There were trees and bushes to climb and even an old bowl to fall asleep in. And always Njinska was nearby, keeping a watchful eye on her family.

The kittens were growing up fast. When they were seven weeks old, it was time to find homes for them. We put a notice in the shop window.

28

It was very sad saying goodbye to all the kittens. But we knew they would make their new owners happy . . . and we still had Njinska, didn't we?